For Anna,
Catherine, and Blythe,
who inspired me to persist, and
for Eli and Georgia, my every day inspiration.
— L.W.
For my parents, Hank and Carol, and
husband Ross, with love and appreciation.
You've helped make my dreams
a reality.
— S.C.

"A Guide for Readers" created by Meredith Moran, Ph.D.

Library of Congress Cataloging-in-Publication Data is available.
Library of Congress Catalog Card Number 2010936998 (Hardcover)

ISBN 978-0-9829938-1-1 (Hardcover)
19 18 17 16 15   2 3 4 5 6 7 8 9 10

ISBN 978-1-939775-11-5 (Paperback)
19 18 17 16 15   1 2 3 4 5 6 7 8 9 10

Printed in USA   First hardcover edition 2010

Little Pickle Press, Inc.
3701 Sacramento Street #494
San Francisco, CA 94118

Please visit us at www.littlepicklepress.com.

Sofia's Dream

By Land Wilson

Illustrated by Sue Cornelison

Little Pickle Press

Sofia was a thoughtful girl,
Who called the moon her giant pearl.

As nights passed and the moon would grow,
She marveled at its opal glow.

One bright night in a dreamy state,
Sofia heard a sound quite late.
As she peeked around at all her toys,
She wondered which one made the noise.

When a beam drew her gaze up high,
She saw a face that winked its eye.

"Hello down there," the moon sang out.
"I hoped to find you peeping out."
"I didn't know the moon could talk."
"Of course I can, I just can't walk."

"I'm very pleased to meet you, Moon.
Can we talk again real soon?"
"If any night I light the sky,
Just say hello and I'll say hi."

From this night on a friendship grew
Into a bond both strong and true.

When her friend was only half in view,
   Sofia asked, "Where's the rest of you?"
If he was just a crescent moon,
   She knew that he might vanish soon.

Then one time when the moon seemed blue,
She noticed that his face was, too.
"Excuse me, Moon, what bothers you?
There must be something I can do."

"You need to come and visit me,
For there is something you must see."
"But you are up there far away!
I'm here on Earth. I have no way."

"My dear friend, let me share with you
Something special that you can do.
Tomorrow night, when you're asleep,
Dream that you take a giant leap."

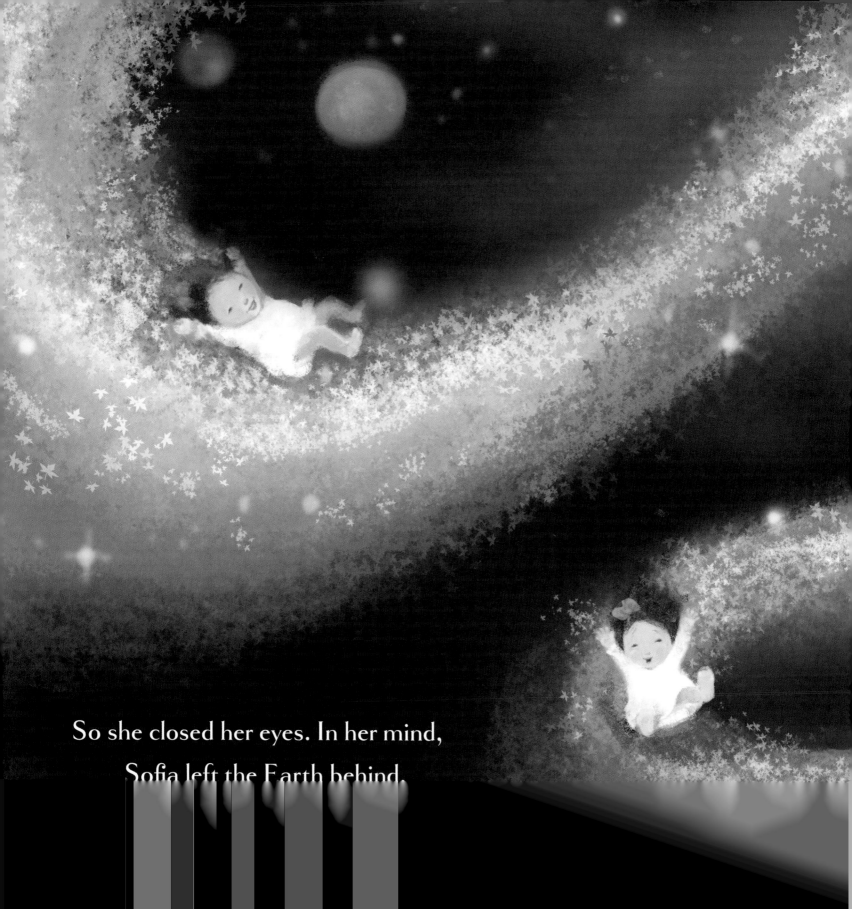

So she closed her eyes. In her mind,

Sofia left the Earth behind.

When she reached the moon in space,
She asked about his gloomy face.
"Now, my friend, that you are here,
I'll show you what it is I fear.
Take a close look at Earth with me,
Then tell me what it is you see."

"There's giant swirls of white and blue.
It's like a marble in our view.
I see such a beautiful place,
Surrounded by the black of space."

"Your Mother Earth is where you live.
 She is my closest relative,
Also home for nature's wonder,
 Now she's saddened by real plunder.

"With dirty waters, land, and air,
 It looks as though she's in despair.
Her people seem so unaware,
 That what Earth needs is better care."

"Why would some want to hurt the place
    Important to my human race?
She is the only home I know,
    Where living things can breathe and grow.

"I see now why you feel so sad.
    An upset mother's very bad.
I wish you were not feeling blue.
    Please tell me, Moon, what should we do?"

"You all must think of Earth each day,
And care for her in every way.
Learn more about what you can do,
To help the Earth and all of you.

"The things you do and what you say,
Will make a difference every day.
Aim high with everything you do,
Then you'll inspire others, too."

"Thank you, Moon,
for the thoughts you share.
It makes good sense. We need to care!
More people need to visit you,
So they can see your point of view."

When Sofia woke up from her dream,
Her cares were different, so it seemed.
Part of the work she pledged to do
Was passing on these words to you:

"One of these nights, I hope quite soon,
  Dream that you leap up to the moon.
There you will find a wise old friend,
  Who has a point of view to lend.

"Once you see from this distant view,
  Awareness may come over you.
By far your gift of greatest worth
  Is our dear home, this planet Earth."

Our Mission

Little Pickle Press is dedicated to helping parents and educators cultivate conscious, responsible little people by stimulating explorations of the meaningful topics of their generation through a variety of media, technologies, and techniques.

Little Pickle Press
Environmental Benefits Statement

This book is printed on Appleton Utopia U2:XG Extra Green Paper. It is made with 30% PCRF (Post-Consumer Recovered Fiber) and Green Power. It is FSC®-certified, acid-free, and ECF (Elemental Chlorine-Free). All of the electricity required to manufacture the paper used to print this book is matched with RECS (Renewable Energy Credits) from Green-e® certified energy sources, primarily wind.

Little Pickle Press saved the following resources by using post-consumer, green-powered paper:

trees	energy	greenhouse gases	wastewater	solid waste
Post-consumer recovered fiber displaces wood fiber with savings translated as trees.	PCRF content displaces energy used to process equivalent virgin fiber.	Measured in CO_2 equivalents, PCRF content and Green Power reduce greenhouse gas emissions.	PCRF content eliminates wastewater needed to process equivalent virgin fiber.	PCRF content eliminates solid waste generated by producing an equivalent amount of virgin fiber through the pulp and paper manufacturing process.
44,000 trees	**31 mil BTUs**	**10,490,000 lbs**	**37,651,000 gal**	**4,060,000 lbs**

Calculations based on research by Environmental Defense Fund and other members of the Paper Task Force; applies to print quanities of 7,500 books.

 B Corporations are a new type of company that use the power of business to solve social and environmental problems. Little Pickle Press is proud to be a Certified B Corporation.

www.littlepicklepress.com

A Guide For Readers

In *Sofia's Dream*, author Land Wilson poetically depicts an ethereal friendship between a young girl and the moon. Through delightful rhyming text and endearing illustrations, children learn to appreciate the Earth as our most precious gift and resource.

Wilson's inspiration for *Sofia's Dream* stems from childhood experiences with conservationist mentors who introduced him to the detrimental effects of human actions on environmental health. Although Wilson's early impassioned efforts to spread environmental awareness were frequently met with unresponsiveness, an adulthood mentor rekindled his sense of commitment to the enviroment and renewed his passion to take action. Wilson subsequently interieved astronauts whose unique perspective on the Earth revealed a striking prevalence of air and water pollution, and a warning for the prolonged health of the Earth and its inhabitants. Captain Walter M. Schirra, Jr. told him, "You realize that humans had better learn to be more careful with this one and only place we need to live." Wilson was propelled to translate this message in a meaningful way for children. And *Sofia's Dream* was born.

Sofia's Dream conveys a series of powerful messages encouraging children to internalize healthy habits of mind and action that promote their own well-being and that of the world they live in, including:

- experiencing the special bond and joy of friendship

- viewing an issue from multiple perspectives

- setting goals and aiming high to reach these goals

- educating oneself about how to care for the Earth
  and fellow beings

- taking action to restore the Earth's beauty and health

- spreading awareness to maintain a strong commitment
  to the Earth's well-being.

Reading *Sofia's Dream* should introduce children to a global perspective on the Earth's natural resources—specifically the air, land, and water—and the interconnected relationship among these resources. This guide includes three projects, one for each of these resources, and should enable children's character development through the pillars of communication, courage, and reasoning. Each project has been designed so that you can build and embellish the activities to a level that best suits the needs of your child. These projects align with the Common Core State Standards Initiative for Speaking and Listening (corestandards.org).

PROJECT #1
Better Care For The World's Air

The air we breathe and the clear skies above provide one of the greatest natural resources on Earth. Unfortunately, this resource is gradually diminishing as a result of toxic emissions produced by the world's vehicles, factories, and industrial production centers. These emissions can create or substantially worsen respiratory conditions. Not only are the toxic emissions harmful to humans, but to animal and plant life as well. Even areas without such emissions are affected as wind can carry pollutants across large distances. Toxic emissions have further contributed to depletion of the stratosphere, or ozone layer, leading to an increase in the level of harmful ultraviolet radiation that reaches the Earth and can eventually cause skin cancer.

Another key component of the Earth's air resources is the sky above. The stars and night sky help regulate the life cycles of both diurnal (i.e., humans) and nocturnal (i.e., raccoons) creatures. Unfortunately, increased light pollution resulting from an over-abundance of artificial light shining into the night sky can be particularly dangerous for many bird species. During migration, birds use the stars as a map to navigate. Excessive artificial light interferes with the birds' ability to follow their natural path and often results in collisions with objects that are rendered invisible because of the light.

TAKE THE PLEDGE!

As citizens of the world, it is both our duty and our right to educate ourselves about the causes and cures for these threats to our natural air resources.

GUIDING QUESTIONS
- Why is the air in our global environment important?
- What are some of our air resources (e.g., atmosphere, ozone layer, sky)?
- What are some living things that inhabit the air?
- What is air pollution? What causes air pollution?
- What is light pollution? What causes light pollution?
- What happens to living things when the air or light they need for survival becomes polluted?

ACTIVITY
Think about the creatures that spend much of their lives in the air (e.g., birds, insects). What happens to these animals when this environment is not cared for properly? Pick an artistic medium (e.g., paint, drawing, role play, poetry) to imagine how these creatures could be impacted when their environmental conditions change. Create different stories of the creatures in both positive and negative environmental conditions.

FOR OLDER READERS
Talk about the environmental protection laws that exist in your community. How do your community's environmental protection laws compare with those of communities around the world? Together, write letters to regional or national legislators encouraging them to adopt more stringent laws regarding environmental protection.

A GROUP PROJECT
Brainstorm ways to help reduce the air and light pollution in your community. As a family, create a pledge to take action to promote healthy air around you. For a sample pledge, visit healthyairliving.com.

CHARACTER BUILDING CONNECTIONS
The key character value to cultivate in this project is courage. Ask children to think about how their thoughts and actions impact the world's air resources:
- What goals can I set for myself to contribute daily to increasing the health of our air?
- How can I persevere in developing a healthy environment even if those around me are not participating in this effort?